You bet it is!

In fact, I never have to wait my turn at all. It's always my turn because I'm an only child.

I ask you, is it fair?

But vacations are the greatest of all! I never have to wait my turn to get a piggyback ride into the ocean, or to paddle the rubber boat, or to sit next to the window in the airplane and watch it take off.

One of the best things is when my parents look at each other and laugh right over my head when I've said something smart or funny—something they've never heard from another kid before. I love to cheer them up!

And when there's a parade, Dad holds *me* on his shoulders so I don't miss anything. He lets me sit on his lap and drive down the driveway, too, and there's only room for one on his knee when he's reading a story or showing me all the stuff in his wallet.

The dog gets to sleep on *my* bed, right on *my* blanket, in *my* room, with no arguments from anyone.

I don't have to fight to watch what I want on Channel Two or Four or Six, either, or get tattled on when I track in mud or forget to brush my teeth.

Then, you should see Christmas! I'm the one who gets to help Dad put the star on top of the tree and leaves a snack for the reindeer and breaks all the eggs into the pudding. And on Christmas morning every package under the tree is —you guessed it—for me!

Of course, if there's an extra biscuit, I get it. I always get the wishbone, the cherry on top of the cake, and the very last sardine, if I want it.

But I'm an only child. At dinner, I'm the only kid at the table, and if something gets spilled, guess who gets the blame? Even if I haven't spilled a thing, if Mom looks sad, or Dad looks as if he's in a bad mood, I keep wondering if it's my fault, and how will I cheer them up?

If I had a sister, I bet she'd return my library books for me and fix my shoelaces so they'd never come untied again.

My brother would cover up for me when I lost my lunch money, race me in his sled, and help me dig a hole to Australia at the beach.

And guess who always has to walk the dog?
I ask you, is that fair?

and when a cereal bowl breaks I get blamed for it, and when the garbage has to get taken out, the leaves have to be raked, the windows have to be washed, I have to do it.

a tag race that lasted through a whole weekend, whispering in bed after the lights were out every single night.

But here I am, an only child,

If I had a brother at home, I could have a pillowfight every Sunday morning, someone to play War with whenever it rained and have snowball fights with whenever it snowed,